The Wim Wom
from the
Mustard Mill

by

Polly Peters

illustrated by

Roberta Angeletti

Published by Child's Play (International) Ltd
Swindon   Auburn ME   Sydney
Text © 2008 Polly Peters   Illustration © 2008 Child's Play (International) Ltd
ISBN 978-1-84643-253-8   www.childs-play.com   Printed in Croatia
1 3 5 7 9 10 8 6 4 2

"Eat your beans," Mom said.
"Or the Wim Wom will want them."

"Pick up those socks," said Dad,
"or the Wim Wom will have them
for ear warmers."

Later, the moment we were in our pajamas,
Mom said, "Bedtime! Quick! Hop in before
the Wim Wom tries your cosy beds for size."

"But MOM!" we said, "What is a WIM WOM?"

She looked surprised. "Why, the Wim Wom
from the Mustard Mill, of course.
Everyone knows about the Wim Wom."

We looked at each other.
"WE don't," we said. But Mom just smiled.

"Of course you do. The Wim Wom
with long ears and round, round eyes."
She kissed us. "Now then, nighty-night.
Sleepy-tight."

And off went the light.

The next morning, we crept downstairs
while everyone was sleeping.
We got out pencils, crayons and paper.

"Do you think a Wim Wom looks like this?"
we asked each other.

When Dad came down, we showed him what we'd drawn.

"Look Dad! Round eyes and long ears.
Is this like a Wim Wom?"

"Mmmmm," he said, looking closely.
"Ah yes! But I think there's something missing.
The Wim Wom from the Mustard Mill also
has two wiggly things on the top of its head."

We looked at each other.
"Two wiggly things?" we said. Dad nodded.

"Now put away those pencils please, or the Wim Wom will tie them to its wiggly things."

Right after breakfast we looked
under the stairs for our big making box.
It was full of all sorts of things we needed.

"This looks useful," we said, poking around,
"and we'll certainly need two of those."

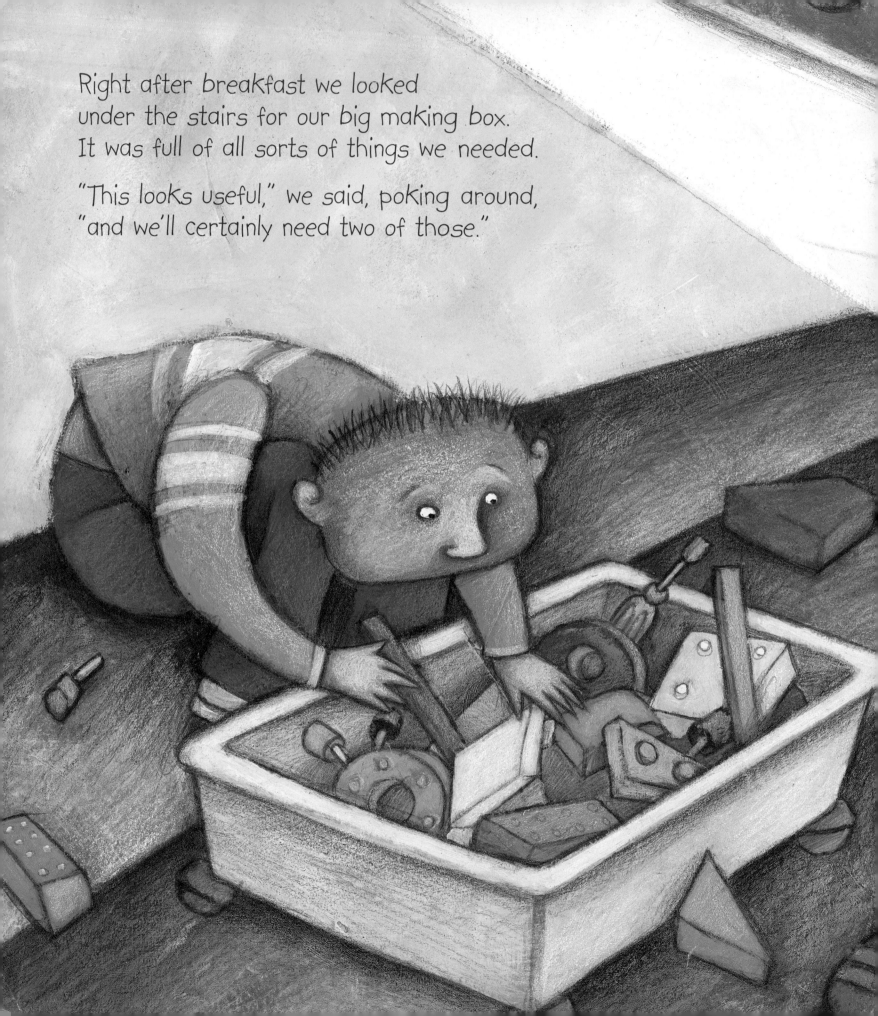

When Grandma came in,
we showed her what we'd made.
"Look Grandma! Round eyes,
long ears AND two wiggly things
on top of its head. Does a Wim Wom
look like this?" we asked.

"Hmmmmm," she said, peering closer.
"Ah yes! But I think there's something missing.
Don't forget its swishy tail."

We looked at each other.
"A swishy tail?" we said.

Grandma nodded. "Now put all that stuff back in the box, or the Wim Wom will want it for a nest."

After lunch, Grandad took us for a walk.
On the way, we collected lots of interesting
things and filled up our pockets.

"Twigs and leaves," we said. "Stones
and long, dry grass. Let's make one now."

Grandad stopped to rest on a bench,
so we played our Wim Wom game.

When it was time to go, we showed him what we'd made.

"Look Grandad! Round eyes, long ears, two wiggly
things on top of its head AND a swishy tail.
Is this what a Wim Wom looks like?"

"Hmmmm," he said, looking down.
"Ah yes! But I think there's something missing.
The Wim Wom from the Mustard Mill also
has a pointy nose."

We looked at each other. "A pointy nose?" we said.

Grandad nodded. "Now, if you want those stones, put them back in your pockets, or the Wim Wom will have them to juggle with."

After supper, Grandma mixed together
flour, salt, water and oil to make us
a big lump of dough. We rolled it out on
the table and squidged it into lots of shapes.

After a while, we showed everyone what we'd made.

"Now look!" we said. "Round eyes, long ears,
two wiggly things on top of its head, a swishy tail
AND a pointy nose. Is THIS what a Wim Wom looks like?"

They looked at each other. "Hmmmmm," they said.
They scratched their heads. "Ah yes! But..."

"What?" we cried. "Is there something missing?"

"Well, actually," said Mom. "To be totally honest,
we're not ABSOLUTELY sure what the Wim Wom looks like."

"But we are experts on what it does!" added Grandad.

"Hmmmmm," we said, staring hard at the grown-ups.
"So, tell us what you DO know about the Wim Wom
from the Mustard Mill."

They were silent for a moment,
then they all spoke in turn.

"The Wim Wom collects any coats
left lying around," said Grandad,
"And uses them to wipe its nose!"

"If you don't make your bed, it uses your sheets for parachutes!" said Grandma.

"It gobbles up any noodles that you leave," said Mom, "and builds a nest with any left over!"

"If you don't tidy away
your toys," said Dad,
"it takes them away,
and uses them to build
Wim Wom space rockets."

We looked at each other.

"What utter RUBBISH!" we laughed.
"You're making it up! It doesn't do any
of those things. We don't believe you!
In fact, we don't believe you really know
anything at all about the Wim Wom."

First Mom smiled, then Dad.
Then suddenly everyone burst out laughing.

With all the noise,
we two were the only ones
who heard a little voice
behind the door.

"Of course that's rubbish,"
it squeaked. "Upon my word,
I've never nibbled noodles
in my life!
Surely EVERYONE knows that
the Wim Wom from the Mustard Mill
only ever eats ICE CREAM!"

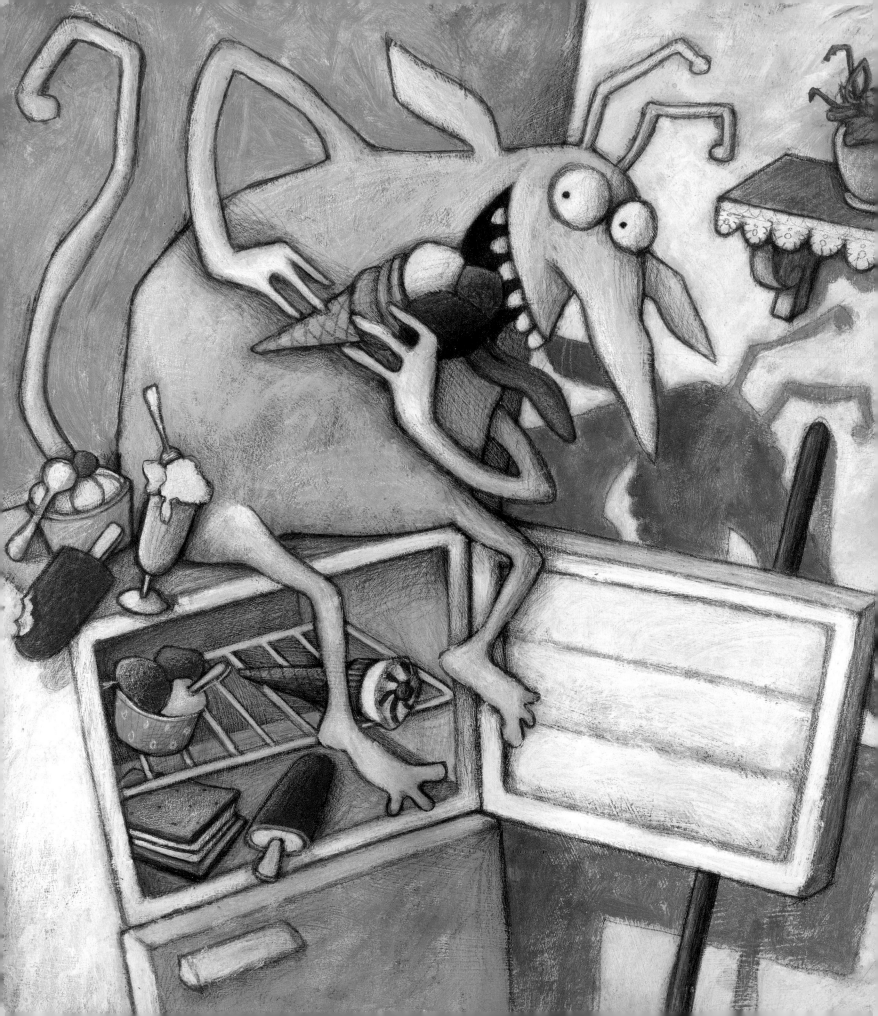